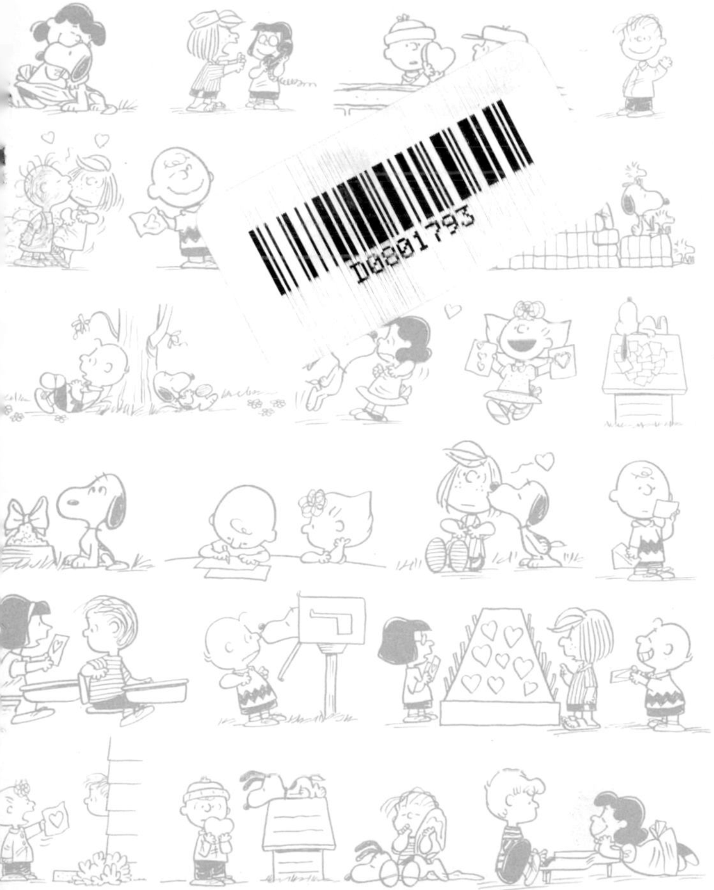

Be
Loving

PEANUTS WISDOM TO CARRY YOU THROUGH

Published by Running Press,
A Member of the Perseus Books Group

Printed in China

Books published by Running Press are available at special discounts for bulk purchases in the United States by corporations, institutions, and other organizations. For more information, please contact the Special Markets Department at the Perseus Books Group, 2300 Chestnut Street, Suite 200, Philadelphia, PA 19103, or call (800) 810-4145, ext. 5000, or e-mail special.markets@perseusbooks.com.

ISBN 978-0-7624-5491-4
Library of Congress Control Number: 2014946117

9 8 7 6 5 4 3 2 1
Digit on the right indicates the number of this printing

Artwork created by Charles M. Schulz
For Charles M. Schulz Creative Associates: pencils by Vicki Scott,
inks by Paige Braddock, colors by Donna Almendrala
Designed by T.L. Bonaddio
Edited by Marlo Scrimizzi
Typography: Archer, Clarendon, Elsie Swash Caps, Gill Sans, Filmotype, Maxwell Slab, Mr Moustache

Running Press Book Publishers
2300 Chestnut Street
Philadelphia, PA 19103-4371

Visit us on the web!
www.runningpress.com
www.snoopy.com

PEANUTS

Be
Loving

PEANUTS WISDOM TO CARRY YOU THROUGH

Based on the comic strip, PEANUTS,
by Charles M. Schulz

RUNNING PRESS
PHILADELPHIA · LONDON

"Love is not knowing what you're talking about."

—*Charles M. Schulz*

Be
VOCAL

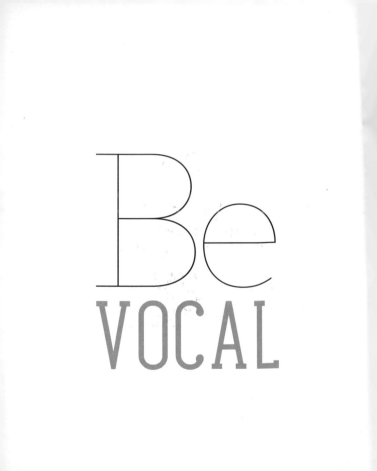

"Thank you . . . and a happy Valentine's Day to you, too!"

—*Snoopy*

Be
Adoring

"You're kind of cute!"

—Lucy

Be
Warm

Be
SINCERE

"Dear Valentine,
    Just a few words to tell you how much I love you.
    I have loved you since the first day I saw you.
    Whenever that was."

        —*Snoopy*

Be
CRAFTY

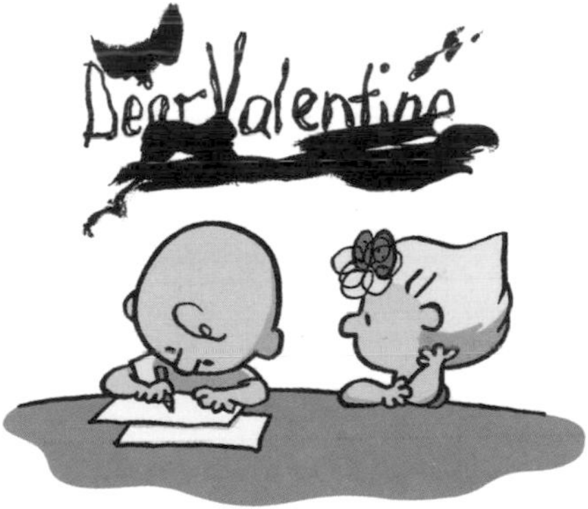
Dear Valentine

Charlie Brown: This year I'm not going to buy any valentines. Instead, I'm going to make my own.

Sally: Who are you sending them to, people you don't like?

Be
Heartfelt

Be
Friendly

Be PASSIONATE

Lucy: Are you going to give me a Valentine?

Schroeder: I never have . . . what makes you think I'll give you one this year?

Lucy: Hope!

Be
Romantic

Sally: Here, Sweet Babboo . . . I brought you a valentine.

Linus: I'm not your sweet babboo!

Sally: Well, take it anyway you blockhead!

Be
CHARMING

"Here, you little doll, you. This valentine is for you. . . ."

—*Charlie Brown*

Be
K-I-S-S-I-N-G

Be
Patient

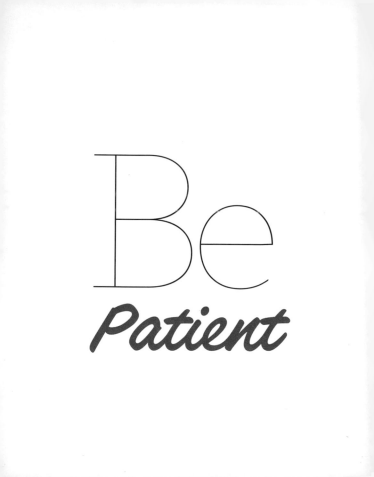

Be

Generous

Lydia: Here, Linus. I want you to have this valentine. But don't misunderstand . . . this doesn't mean I love you or anything.

Linus: What does it mean?

Lydia: It means I happened to have an extra one left over.

Be
STEADFAST

"Dear Contributor,
Thank you for submitting your valentine. We
regret to inform you that it does not suit our
present needs."

Be

Kind

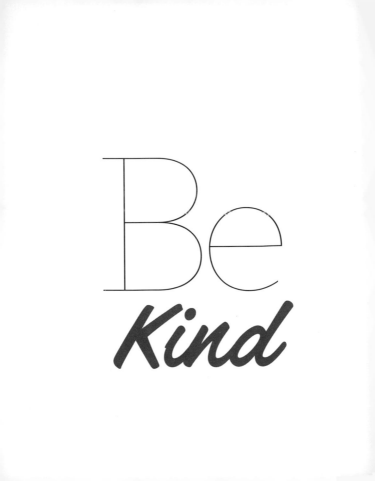

Be
THOUGHTFUL

Linus: Here, I made you a valentine. See? I wrote a little poem, and then I drew some hearts around it.

Lydia: It's in black and white.

Be
Cute

"How come you've never asked me what it's like to be the cutest of the cute?"

—*Lucy*

Be
BOLD

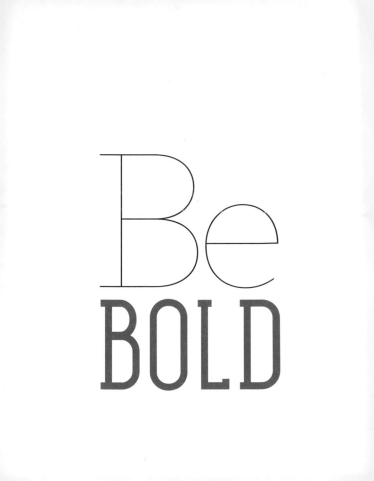

Marcie: We just called to say goodbye, Charles. We're going to miss you . . . we love you.

Peppermint Patty: MARCIE!

Be
Playful

Linus: Did you go to the eye doctor yesterday?

Charlie Brown: Yes, he said there's nothing wrong with my eyes ... they're fine.

Linus: Did he tell you to stop winking at girls?

Be
Excited

Sally: He's hanging around the candy store trying to decide what to get me.... It'll probably be a box of candy shaped like a big heart.

Linus: Or a big ZERO!

Sally: Isn't he the cutest thing?

Be
INFATUATED

Charlie Brown: I wonder if it's possible to be in love with two different girls at the same time.

Snoopy: I remember once when I had two cookies . . . a chocolate chip and a peanut butter . . . and I loved them both.

Be
Touching

Linus: Here, Sally . . . happy Valentine's Day.

Sally: Excuse me, a tear came to my eye!

Be
A TEAM

Be
TENDER

"Love makes you do strange things."

—*Charlie Brown*

Be
Close

Be
Precious

"This one is for 'my sweet babboo' and this one is for 'the cutest of the cute.'"

—*Sally*

Be

Mushy

Be
Gushy

Be
Sweet

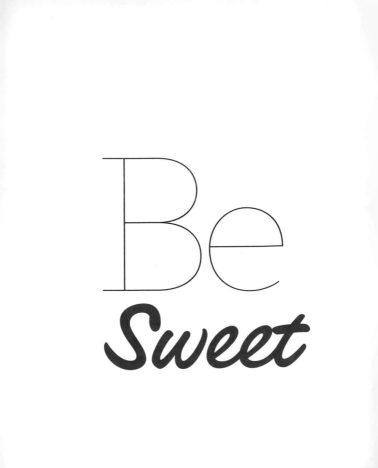

Charlie Brown: I bought this valentine candy for the little red haired girl, but I was too shy to give it to her . . . I'd give it to you, but chocolate isn't good for dogs.

Snoopy: I could just pick out the caramels.

Be

AFFECTIONATE

Be
Particular

Marcie: Sir, are you going to give a valentine to Charles?

Peppermint Patty: I don't know. I hate to waste a valentine on someone I can strike out on three straight pitches.

Be
LOVEY

Be
DOVEY

Be

Brave

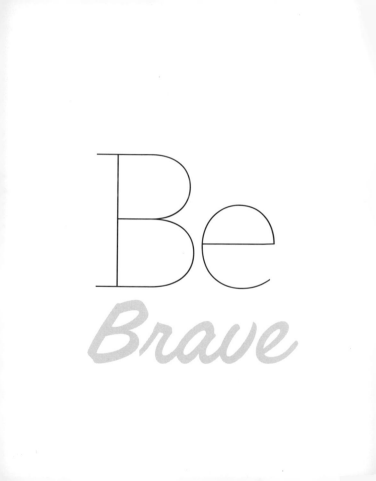

Charlie Brown: Why couldn't I have given her the box of candy and said, "Here, this is for you. I love you"? Why couldn't I have done that?

Linus: Because you're you, Charlie Brown.

Be
Clever

Be

TOGETHER

Be
Mine!

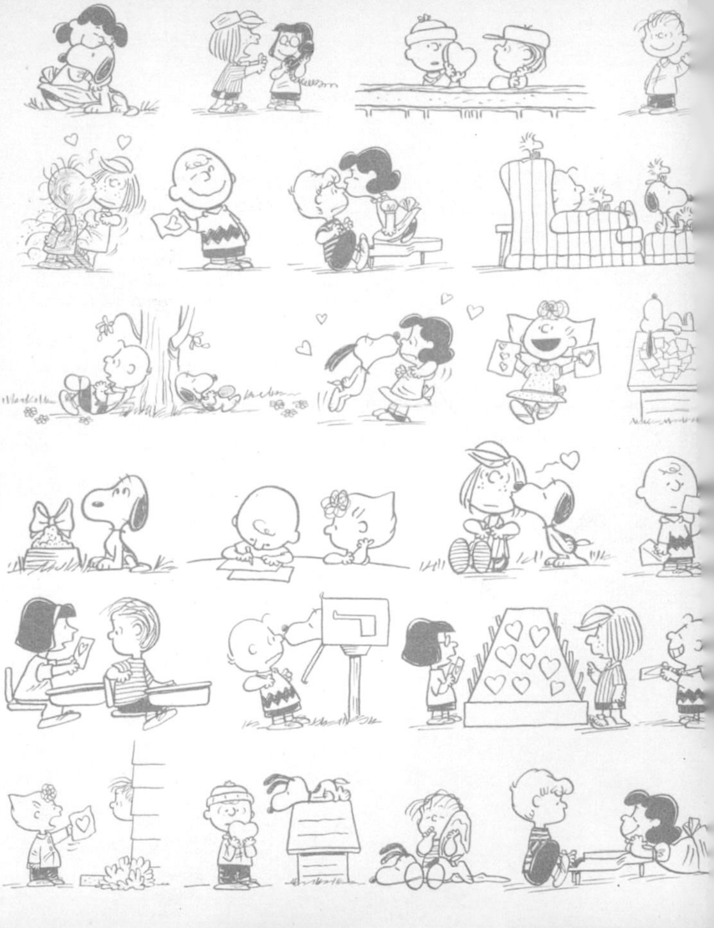